Shattered Heart

ENCHANTED WISHES COLLECTION

VIOLA TEMPEST

VIOLA TEMPEST PUBLISHING

Copyright

Shattered Heart

Enchanted Wishes Collection

© Copyright 2023 Viola Tempest

Cover Design by Fay Lane Cover Design

Contents

Shattered HEART

ENCHANTED WISHES COLLECTION

VIOLA TEMPEST

Chapter One

Chris drummed his fingers on the steering wheel as he waited for the standstill traffic to come back up to a slow crawl. After a grueling day at work, he was eager to get home to his fiancé. He imagined she had dinner prepared for him, as she usually did. As a professional chef, she graced him daily with her decadent, expert meals.

When he finally pulled around the corner into his driveway and stepped through the front door, he found an empty living room. He smelled nothing cooking from the kitchen, and when he wandered in there, he found it empty.

"Leah?" he called out.

He heard the shuffling of rushed footsteps on the stairs and glanced through the living room to find her panting at the bottom of the steps.

"Chris," she said. "You're home early."

Bewilderment knit his brows together. He glanced down at his wristwatch.

"No, I'm not," he said. "I'm ten minutes late."

Leah stared at him expectantly, like he was supposed to say something else. There was a strange contortion on her features, something frazzled and flustered.

"Are you alright?" he pressed, treading through the living room to peer closer at her face. He sensed something amiss.

She nodded and backed away from him as he reached towards her face.

"I'm fine," she said, her words hurried and slurred together. "I'm sorry I lost track of time. Let me get dinner going for you."

She darted around him and slipped into the kitchen. Chris was left standing in the living room alone, listening to the rattling sound of pots and pans in the kitchen. He heard the gas click on the stove and frowned.

Chris had known Leah since they were only fourteen. He knew her well and could tell that something was not right. Concerned, he followed her into the kitchen and came to stand behind her at the stove. His hands fell to her hips, like they had so many times before.

But instead of leaning back into his touch like she usually did, Leah slipped out of the circle of his arms and moved to the kitchen sink.

"Leah, is something bothering you?" he asked, watching her flit around the kitchen like a bee, wielding knives, stirring pots, and washing vegetables.

She refused to look at him as she bustled around, keeping her head low to her chest. Chris began to feel a sickening, burbling dread sloshing around in his stomach.

"I told you I'm fine, Chris," she insisted.

He gave her a disbelieving look that she did not catch. She continued to ignore him as she cooked, and Chris got the hint that she wanted to be left alone.

It wasn't that peculiar that she occasionally had a mood. They have had their difficulties in the decade that they'd known each other, but they were in a good place now. A happy place. Leah was the light of his life.

Without her, he never would have made it through his computer science degree. He never would have survived his father's funeral or the financial struggles they found themselves in throughout college.

She was his steady rock, but he was aware that sometimes people needed a break from each other. Though they had hardly spent much time together since she started her new job at the five-star restaurant downtown, Chris understood why she might need some alone time. He'd never worked in a restaurant before, but he could imagine the stress.

"Alright, I'm just going to head upstairs and change," he said, giving her a sidelong glance as he made his way to the stairs.

He saw her whip around to look at him for the first time since she went into the kitchen. Her eyes were wide, and her lips were pressed in a tight line. She said nothing, but he was not blind to the worry on her face.

The dread sluicing through his stomach began to boil over. He thought he might vomit when he heard a thudding noise coming from the bedroom. Panic seized his chest. He rushed into the bedroom, just in time to see a nude man leaping from the second story window.

Chris ran to the windowsill and watched the man scurry across the grass.

"Hey!" he called after the man, but it was too late.

Chris watched him scamper to a car parked a few houses down.

Trembling with fury and disbelief, Chris stumbled his way back to the kitchen. Leah was standing at the stove, her head down over the pot she was simmering.

"Leah," he snapped. "Who was that upstairs?"

When she turned to face him, there were already tears streaming down her face. He saw the quiver of her lower lip, and he moved around the table to look into her eyes. He needed to see her clearly when he demanded the truth from her.

"I'm sorry, Chris," she whispered.

She fiddled with the engagement ring on her fingers, twisting it up and down her knuckle. His gaze was drawn to the meager diamond he had saved up for so long to afford for her, the best symbol of his love that he had to offer.

"You're cheating on me," he said in disbelief, feeling his eyes growing hot.

"Chris, you know things have been rocky between us for a while," she said with a trembling voice. Somewhere beneath her quivering girlishness, he sensed her frustration.

"They have?" he asked dryly. "I wasn't aware."

"Please," she begged. "We never see each other anymore, and... I don't know. I just feel like we've both changed so much. I know I'm not the girl I was when I was fourteen. My world had always been so small, and when I'm with—"

She cut herself off and averted her gaze. Her arms were crossed in a tight knot over her chest as she drew herself as small as she could against the stove.

"With who?" he asked. "Who was he? What's his name? I want to know."

Leah sniffled and reached behind her to turn off the stove. He gave her a moment to collect herself, seeing the trepidation evident on her face. But as she chewed her lower lip, he realized she had no intention of telling him.

"Do you love this guy, Leah?" he demanded, the hot prickling in his eyes starting to form tears that pooled beneath his lids without falling.

She wiped at the tears on her cheeks with her sleeve and then fixed him with a stern look that brooked no room for argument.

"I think we should break up," she finally said. "I'm so sorry to have hurt you, Chris. I *do* care about you, I really do. I just want to experience more of what's out there. We're still so young, and I just don't think I'm ready for marriage."

Chris blinked at her, the realization still sinking in.

"You're the love of my life, Leah," he said. "I want to make this work. That other guy? We can forget about that. Let's not throw our relationship away because of one mistake."

"It wasn't a mistake."

Chris recoiled as if he'd been bitten. An unearthly silence settled over the kitchen. The pot on the stove was spewing up its last simmering bubbles. It was so quiet that Chris could hear the tick of his wristwatch and the low rattle of Leah's breathing.

"Not a mistake to cheat on me?" he asked, finally breaking the tense silence.

Leah shook her head, her brown eyes glimmering with a fresh wave of tears.

"That's not what I meant," she explained with a watery voice. "It was wrong of me. I know that, but I don't think breaking up with you is a mistake. I really think this is for the best."

Chris swallowed the lump in his throat and sucked in a deep breath for composure. Their lives were so deeply intertwined that he couldn't even entertain the idea of a breakup.

"You're not thinking straight, Leah," he said. "Let's sleep on it. We can discuss this again in the morning when you've got a clear head."

"I've got a clear head now, Chris," she snapped. "Listen to what I'm telling you. This is over between us. I hate to hurt you like this, but it's really over."

She reached again for the engagement ring on her

finger and twisted it over her knuckle. Chris shook his head while she stared at the ring in her open palm. He saw the hesitancy on her face, the window of opportunity.

"Do not give me the ring back, Leah," he commanded. "We can fix this."

With a sob, she pressed the ring into his hand. She closed her palms around his and leaned up to press a chaste kiss on his mouth. He felt the tremble of her lips against his and drew in a shaky breath. His breath felt tight in his chest, like he could not fill his lungs up with the right amount of air.

"I'm sorry, Chris."

Chapter Two

For the next few agonizing days, Chris was a listless ghost drifting through his life. At work, he got his tasks done efficiently, with a glazed unfeeling kind of focus, like he was numb to the entire world around him. He had shed no tears since Leah left that evening with a single packed suitcase loaded into the sedan he had bought for her.

She came into the house when he was away. He knew this because her things gradually disappeared – the collection of makeup and jewelry on the dresser, the stack of trashy romance novels by the television, even the hamster wheel belonging to their shared pet who had died years ago was missing from its dusty corner in the garage.

The day that there were no vestiges of her left in the house, Chris came home from work to find her key sitting on the kitchen counter. For a while, he did not move it, refusing to cement the devastating breakup by relegating it to a spare key to be stuffed in the junk drawer. It just didn't seem right.

After a week, Chris was a hopeless mess. He had trouble finding the motivation to pull himself out of bed each morning and go to work. Even mundane tasks were difficult to manage.

In a moment of weakness, he brought out his laptop and pulled up Leah's social media profile. He almost at once regretted the decision when he saw that she had officially moved into another man's house. He recognized the ginger-haired man as the same one who had jumped from his bedroom window.

Bradley was the name tagged in the picture of him and Leah at the bowling alley with matching, corny collared shirts. Revolted, he slammed the laptop shut.

He couldn't understand how she could so easily throw away everything they had built together, all for some guy named *Bradley.*

It didn't seem fair. He had always been the perfect boyfriend. He never forgot a birthday or anniversary, always noticed when she got her hair cut or bought a new lipstick. He had done everything right, so why had she left him anyway?

Though he struggled to see her perspective in things, it wasn't as though he never had a wandering eye. It's just that when he saw a beautiful woman, he thought of her as nothing more than that. She could never compare to Leah – no woman could.

But if she seemed to think that there could be something better out there for her, perhaps, there could be something better out there for *him* as well.

For the first time in a week, Chris busted out his beard-trimmer. He styled his dark curls with some sweet-smelling mousse and dabbed a little cologne on his neck. It had been a while since he had dressed up to go out, so when he stood in front of his closet of work suits, he was not sure how to present himself for nightlife.

Eventually, he settled on a simple white button-down and a pair of slacks and headed out into the night.

The weekend's bustling spirit was high on the crowded streets. Chris wove his way through the quaint downtown cobblestone sidewalk, looking for a relatively calm, uncrowded bar where he could sit and relax.

It would be nice to enjoy a cold beer and know that he was free to flirt with any beautiful woman he might meet.

He found an alehouse on a street corner and took a seat at the bar. The air inside was smokey and humid, filled with the thrumming low chords of an acoustic guitar being played on the small stage.

Chris ordered a beer and glanced around the bar as he sipped. There were a few people dancing by the stage, and half the tables were filled with bobbing patrons nursing at their fruity drinks. Chris scanned their faces, unsure of how to proceed.

He had been out of the dating game since he was fourteen. It was safe to say that his skills were a little rusty, that he had no clue how to pick up a woman.

Fortunately for Chris, he was blessed to be considered conventionally attractive, growing into his aristocratic features as he aged. Though he always appeared gaunt as a child, by the time he had graduated from college, his reputation for rejecting women across campus had given him the perhaps undeserved title of *ineligible bachelor*.

Leah had always been a bit of a heartbreaker as well, and Chris had been so proud of their status as a power couple back then.

Even looking at the crowd of women in the bar, he couldn't find a single one as beautiful as Leah. None of them radiated her charm or grace. There was something magnetic and alluring about Leah that no one else on Earth seemed to have.

Chris choked back the rest of his beer, hoping it would drown the urge he felt to cry. He may have never picked up a woman at a bar before, but he was pretty sure the best way to do it wasn't bursting into tears over his ex.

He regretted his decision to come here tonight. The results could easily have been predicted if he had just thought for one moment, not acted on raw, jealous instinct. He could not simply waltz into a bar and find a woman of equal caliber to Leah.

He knew the things he loved most about Leah were not things that he could gauge just from appearance. Though his eyes were drawn to the blondes in the room, particularly the ones with the same honey wheat shade as Leah's locks, he knew that the warmth and compassion and empathy he sought were not hiding beneath blonde hair or brown eyes.

They could be in any of these women, and all he had to do was choose one to make a move on. Just a simple introduction, a polite conversation. He could do that, couldn't he?

But his legs didn't want to obey his brain. They twitched and bounced, perched on the scaffold beneath the barstool. He flagged down the bartender and ordered another drink, hoping the alcohol would dilute his reserved nature.

Deep down, he already knew he wouldn't be leaving here with a woman tonight. It wasn't in the cards for him. He didn't even want another woman if he was honest with himself. He just wanted to prove that he could move on as quickly as Leah apparently had.

But when he went home that night to fall asleep in the bed that they used to share, he knew that he wouldn't be getting over her any time soon. At least not while he's living in the house they were supposed to start their married life in.

All he could see when he looked around the quaint, two-story townhouse were the absent voids of Leah's things, the clean ring in the dust on the mantle where her favorite Tiffany lamp used to sit, the empty magnetic knife rack glinting above the kitchen sink.

There was no way he could get over Leah in this place. He needed more space, a continent or an ocean between them, a place untouched by her presence. He couldn't continue on like this with his emotions roiling, threatening to burble over and destroy him.

15

Chapter Three

The next morning, he called out of work. He told them he'd be taking a week of his vacation days and booked a plane ride to Phuket. It was a somewhat impulsive choice to go to Thailand, but the fare was reasonably priced, and he knew that it was a beautiful place with stunning white beaches and glimmering lagoons, the perfect place to get away.

He found a hotel near the bustling markets, and when he finally deboarded the plane and checked into his room, he felt his first sense of balance since the breakup.

The air in Thailand was humid, with the tang of salt drifting off the sea. The sun was just beginning to set as Chris ventured out into Phuket's famous night market. Despite his jetlag, he felt a burst of energy and adventure as he strolled through the colorful tents and brightly lit market stalls. The sweet scent of baked pastries lingered in the air, and the advertising call of vendors rang from every corner of the street.

Chris wandered along with no rhyme or reason, stopping at boiled candy carts and sea glass trinket stalls. He had a mouthful of lemon candy when he heard the persistent shouts of an old woman to his right.

He glanced over and found her beckoning to him, her eyes wild. At first, he was confused, did not understand that she was gesturing to *him*. He looked around and realized that he was the one she was speaking to.

"Yes, you," she croaked with a thick accent. "Come to me. I have something for you."

"Something for me?" he asked, bewildered as he took a step closer.

She was standing behind a stall of glittering trinkets, with some ornate amulets hanging from long chains and jeweled bangles stacked in tidy columns. She moved beneath the counter of her stall, and when she stood again, she was holding a rather ordinary-looking wooden box.

"I sense it in your spirit," she said vaguely, waving her arm to beckon him even closer.

Chris obliged and stepped close enough to peer inside the box as she tilted the lid open.

"My spirit?" he asked.

The woman glanced up at him with her wizened, wrinkled eyes. She reached ominously into the box, and beneath the folds of white silk that cradled the tiny glass stone object, she pulled it from its depths.

"Your spirit," she confirmed. "Your loneliness. It's so intense I could feel it the moment you stepped into the market."

"Really?" Chris asked dryly, staring at the small, heart-shaped stone in her palm.

"This wasn't an ordinary shop, boy," she replied. "I know you're American, so I'll forgive your lack of manners. All the items in my shop have a fate, a set owner. I'm just the purveyor of the message."

He gave her a skeptical glance. "And what message would that be?"

"It's different for every person," she said, returning

his dubious look with one of her own. "For you, this heart stone was fated. I heard it calling for you. With this heart stone in your pocket, your troubles with loneliness will be over. You will have much luck in love."

Chris did not believe the tall tale. He reached to pluck the stone from her palm and twisted it around with his fingers, checking every angle to see if it was truly something out of the ordinary. It appeared nothing more than a carved piece of glass, but he had to admit that it had a satisfying weight in the palm of his hand.

"I'm sorry," he said to her. "I think I'm going to have to pass."

He tried to press the stone back into her hand, but she stepped away from him and refused to accept it. She shook her head vigorously, throwing her hands up into the air.

"You must take it," she said. "You must. It calls to you. It wanted *you.* Do you understand? There will be other forces to reckon with if you do not accept your fate."

Chris blinked at her. "Other forces?"

"Strong forces," she said emphatically. "To appease them, you must buy the heart stone and keep it on your person."

He gave her a roving glance, wondering how many

tourists this woman had tricked into buying her useless tchotchkes.

"I must buy it?" he asked in challenge.

She nodded. Chris tossed the stone into the air and caught it, testing its weight in his palm. The woman's face pulled into a peach-pit wince, and he realized that even if it wasn't true, she did believe what she was saying with some degree of conviction.

"Fine," he said, pulling out his wallet and handing her a stack of bills. As he was counting the money, he took pity on the elderly women and added a few extra bills to the stack he passed over to her.

"Remember to keep it in your pocket," she urged as she stuffed the money into a drawer under the counter. "It won't work unless you keep it in your pocket."

Chris slipped his wallet back into his pocket, eyeing her one more time.

"How exactly is it supposed to work?" he asked.

She gave him a grim, harrowing smile. "You'll see."

Chapter Four

Chris slept well that night. If he had any dreams, he could not remember them, and when he woke in his hotel room, he felt refreshed and ready to take on Thailand.

The first order of business on his itinerary was a solo kayak through the Phang Nga Bay. He had always wanted to kayak or go white-water rafting, but when he had planned trips with Leah, she always resisted his more athletic and outdoorsy suggestions, much to his chagrin. She was more than happy to indulge him in some things, but kayaking had never been one of them.

Now, he had the chance to do all the things he could never do with Leah. He could hardly imagine her willingly kayaking into Phuket's dark sea caves, but just the idea of it sent a thrill of anticipation down his spine.

Before he left his hotel room, Chris glanced at the heart stone he had left on the bathroom counter. It sat beside the soap dispenser, ordinary and unremarkable. He didn't think it was capable of anything mystical or otherworldly, but like a totem or a palm stone, he found comfort in squeezing it in his fist.

So, he tucked it into his pocket before he made his way down to the pier and rented a kayak to take out onto the water.

With a map of the caves in one pocket and the heart stone in the other, Chris took his paddles and shoved out into the sea. The waves were gentle, lapping with tender ebbs at the white shore. The sky above was cloudless and blue, nearly too blinding to look at.

Despite the amount of tourists he saw at the crowded pier, the water was calm and quiet as he pulled out his map and set course for the first entrance into the caves. He was warned that they could be labyrinthian, and that he needed to pay close attention to his map or get hopelessly lost.

The first towering structure of rock pierced the sky in the distance, stark against the bright sunlight. Chris floated through its shadow, letting the cool air wash over him as he neared the mouth of the cave.

Mangroves lined the cavern's entrance, their roots spiraling in and out of the water in complex twists and whirls. Chris was careful to keep his paddle clear of them as he rowed through the narrow canal and into the chilly cave.

He repressed a shiver as the darkness slowly enveloped him. He could still see the blue glow of the water beneath the kayak and a pinprick of light in the distance that marked the cave's exit. As his vision adjusted, the mossy walls of the cavern come into focus.

There was something ethereal about the place, like a sensory deprivation tank where he was somehow even more acutely aware of all his pain. There was nothing else to feel in here but the dank chill in the air, and Chris felt the sudden urge to lean over the side of the kayak and vomit into the sea.

He managed to keep his breakfast down and his paddles steady. The water was smooth beneath the wide blade of his paddle, and he focused on the physical sensation of driving the kayak forward rather than the jumbled thoughts tumbling through his mind.

At some point while rowing along, the pinprick of light in the distance disappeared. Chris's vision grew darker and darker the further he slinked into the cave. When he glanced behind him, he saw nothing but a black void, an emptiness that threatened to swallow him whole.

Panic filled his throat, clenching his heart so that each pounding pump of blood through his veins expanded it against his aching ribcage. His breath came in shallow pants. Without his sight, he couldn't navigate the caves, couldn't tell where he was going. His map was of little use to him here, and he felt growing dread burgeoning in his stomach.

Instinctively, he patted his pants, fumbling around for the heart stone. As silly as it was, he thought it might calm him down to hold it.

It was then that he noticed a faint glow emanating from his pocket. Startled, he fished into his pocket and removed the source of light.

The heart stone glowed in his palm, a bright, pulsing white light that crescendoed and mounted, cutting blinding rays into the darkness around him. He had to look away from it as his eyes began to sting and water. The stone was warm in his hands, almost hot. If he wasn't so afraid to lose it, he would have thrown it into the water.

As the light grew brighter and brighter, Chris felt it growing hotter and hotter in his hand, until he dropped it into the seat of his kayak. He squeezed his eyes shut, blinded by the intensity of the heart stone's light.

A mechanical whirring sound filled the air, shrill and piercing. Chris winced and buried his face in his hands. He didn't know what was happening, and the fear prickled at his skin, coating it with sharp goosebumps.

He could feel the heat of the heart stone in his lap, and he sensed that the light was dwindling. When the pinkness of his eyelids returned to black, he blinked his eyes open and stared into his lap. The heart stone was still there, its glow faded but still present.

But now, there was another glow in the cave, something ghostlike and wispy, floating across the surface of the water. At first, Chris thought it was just a shapeless white blob, like a formless entity.

It skimmed the water a few feet away from the boat, and as it turned, Chris saw that it was a woman cloaked in gossamer white silk, standing on the water.

At first, he believed he was looking into the face of God. What other explanation was there for this strange woman, this ethereal glow in the dark cave? She was not a creature of this earth, and he could tell just by looking at her.

He wondered though, if God was supposed to have a face like Leah's. Surely, it could not be a coincidence that this angelic woman had the same rich chestnut eyes as Leah.

It was *not* Leah, though. There were differences that he could see even from this distance. Her brows were darker and straighter, her nose a little more sloped. She was no less beautiful than Leah, which was the first time Chris had thought that about someone since he was fourteen.

"Hello?" he called out to the apparition, his voice cracking.

The woman glided closer to him, her stature poised and elegant.

"Hello," she replied, her gaze falling on him for the first time. Her voice was silky smooth and crystal clear, like a chime ringing out through the silence.

"Who are you?" he asked, his knuckles white around the grip of the paddle."

Chapter Five

She tilted her head at him. He watched the smooth tresses of her auburn hair glide over her shoulders. Her lips curled into a soft smile, one that was patient and kind.

"I am whoever you want me to be, Chris," she said. "You've released me from the heart stone. I must have fallen into your possession for a reason."

Chris blinked at her. He was sure now that he was dreaming.

"You know my name?" he asked her.

She nodded at him, gesturing towards the glowing stone in his lap.

"We are joined together now," she replied. "I am yours."

"Mine?" he asked incredulously. "I don't understand. I still don't know who you are or how you got here. You live in this stone?"

He plucked the stone up from where it sat between his legs and closed his fingers around it. He felt an energy coursing through it, something potent and powerful, though he couldn't quite describe the sensation. Nevertheless, it was something tangible, something beyond belief. He had never been a superstitious person, or the kind of man to subscribe to any supernatural notions. This, however, was undeniable. He had visual proof that there was something other-worldly about this simple piece of glass.

"My name is Serena," she said.

Chris did not know why he half-expected her to say her name was Leah. Something about her was undeniably Leah-like.

"Come here, Serena," he said, assessing the 'ownership' she claimed he had over her.

Obediently, the woman came closer, her lithe legs

moving fluidly beneath the sheer silk of her gown. Ripples splayed beneath her footsteps, leaving glowing footprints in their wake on the surface of the water. Mesmerized, Chris watched with wide eyes as she neared the edge of the kayak and knelt down beside him.

Hesitantly, he reached towards her face, expecting that his fingers would move right through her. Instead, the tips of his fingers contacted the impossibly soft skin of her cheek. He felt a shock of electricity course through him at the touch and recoiled.

"Are you lost, Chris?" she asked.

He wasn't sure if she was talking in a metaphysical sense, but either way, his answer was the same. He nodded.

"Put me back into the heart stone," she said, "and I will guide you through the caves."

Chris gave her a dubious look. Part of him wondered if he had succumbed to the insanity of his loneliness. He could not help but feel like he would wake up at any moment. It almost sucked the sense of danger out of the situation, though his body still reacted with sweat and a pounding heart.

"How do I put you back into the stone?" he asked.

She put her hand beneath his where he cupped the stone and lifted it up so that he was holding it at chest level.

"I will touch the stone and go back inside," she explained to him, her eyes glimmering when they connected with his. The eye contact was more exhilarating than the feel of her skin against his. He felt it like an arrow to his heart.

As she moved to touch the stone, Chris pulled it out of arm's reach.

"How will I get you back out again?" he asked. "How could you guide me from inside the stone? I couldn't see anything in the darkness."

Serena smiled at him again, and the sight made butterflies flurry up in his stomach.

"To call for me, simply kiss the stone," she said. "I will be waiting for you."

She reached for the stone again, this time, too quickly for Chris to snatch it away. He was not yet ready for her to disappear. If it was all just a dream, he was not ready to wake up.

But when her fingers came into contact with the heart-shaped stone in his palm, the blinding light returned, spreading, expanding, consuming the darkness of the cave with vigor and frenzy. Chris knew light could not be *heard*, yet, it rattled in his teeth and applied tense pressure to his eardrums like he had been plunged deep underwater.

A cry teared from his throat, though he wasn't exactly sure what he was overcome with that made him shout in such a raw and visceral way. He buried his face in his hands, waiting for the worst of it to be over.

When he finally opened his eyes again, the woman was gone. The cave was cast in total darkness so that his eyes may well have been closed. After a beat, when nothing happened, Chris released a breath he hadn't realized he was holding in.

Surely, it was all an illusion, a figment of his imagination. The adventure of being in a new country, of suffering through a breakup, of all his culminating feelings that he couldn't control, must have skewed his mind, given him silly visions.

He shook his head to clear his mind, desperately confused. His hands were still trembling as he began to row through the dark water. He was only a few strokes into his blind journey when the light sprung back to the stone.

This time, instead of a warm, emanating glow, the stone shone a beam of targeted light out into the darkness, a single ray shining like a spotlight towards the murky water off in the distance.

With little choice, Chris rowed the kayak through the beam of light. The stone sat precariously on his knee like a little guiding star. As his kayak glided through the water, the light moved and waned, pointing out the best path for him to take.

It was not long before the pinprick of the cave's

exit appeared in the distance. Chris picked up his pace, rowing quickly towards the light, feeling a weight lift off his shoulders as it got brighter and brighter.

Soon, he could see the leafy mangrove trees that lined the exit, and the dappled rays of sunshine that peeked through the canopy into the calm water.

It was with rejuvenating relief that he finally pushed the kayak back out into the open water, away from the murky, mossy, entrapping walls of the caverns. The sun warmed the chill that had lodged a place in his bones, and his heart resumed a normal pace. His lungs felt less tight in his chest, the air so clean and refreshing in his chest.

Out in the direct sunlight, Chris glanced down at the stone sitting on his knee. It was unmarkable now, no glow coming from the porous stone. Instead, it appeared just as ordinary as it had when the old woman had feverishly pressed it into his hands.

He was now more certain than ever that the whole ordeal had been nothing more than a wild figment of his desperate imagination. Surely, that ghostly woman had just been his own mind trying to fight for his survival. It had been his *own* instinct guiding him out of the cave, and it was ridiculous to think otherwise.

Still, Chris could not help but feel a little shaken as he returned his rented kayak and headed back to his hotel for the evening. Though there were still a few hours of sunlight left, Chris didn't have it in him to enjoy any more activities for the day.

When he was back in his room, sitting on his hotel bed, Chris set the heart stone down beside him and stared. He could not decide whether it would bring him good luck or bad luck to keep it. He wasn't sure he even believed in luck and had half a mind to return it to the old woman.

But there was something comforting about having it on his person. Despite his lack of superstition, he clutched the stone in his clenched fist as he laid back against the pillow and drifted off into a deep, dreamless sleep.

Chapter Six

The next morning when Chris woke, the stone was still cradled in his palm. It was hot, but not unnaturally so, just the residual heat from his body melted into the rock. He gave it a cursory squeeze, and then tossed it in a short arc up into the air so he could catch it again.

He had a few more adventures planned before he left Thailand, and on today's agenda, was an elephant ride through Phuket's famous animal sanctuary. Elephants had always been Leah's favorite animal. They had seen them at the zoo before, but Leah was much too afraid to ever attempt to ride on one.

There was nothing stopping him from riding one now, so Chris dressed in comfortable clothes for the heat and slipped the heart stone into his pocket before he made his way down to the street to hail a cab.

By the time he arrived at the animal sanctuary, the sun was high in the early afternoon sky, beaming fiercely down onto the sandy earth beneath him. He found the guide he had booked online amidst the crowd of tourists and was led into a small enclosure with a single elephant inside.

It was smaller than the elephants he remembered from the zoo back at home, but no less impressive up close. The scent of manure and cut grass was acrid in the air, more potent as he stepped towards the wrinkly, grey elephant.

His guide instructed him to pet just the trunk with a gentle, open palm. Hesitantly, Chris stepped forward and put his hand on the elephant's trunk and gave it a few tender strokes.

There was a magnetic, compelling quality to the

elephant's wise, black eyes. It made Chris's chest swell with a feeling he couldn't quite describe, something open and childlike, receptive to the world in an unencumbered way.

The elephant's trunk extended outward, reaching for Chris's other hand, the one where he held a large carrot the guide had given him. Obligingly, Chris tossed the carrot up into the air for the elephant to catch with her massive trunk before pulling it into her mouth.

Delighted, Chris asked the guide if he could ride the elephant alone. He wanted to experience what it was like to be alone with this powerful creature, wandering through nature on its back.

The guide was hesitant at first, but when Chris spoke the universal language of money, he allowed Chris to climb up solo onto the elephant's saddle. Chris seated himself in the short-walled carriage that enclosed the saddle and took up the reigns.

It was harrowing to have such a massive and powerful animal between his legs. As she began to take her first slow, ambling steps, Chris felt a grin spread across his face. The noise of the tourism faded away as he trekked deeper into the sandy woods.

After his experience in the caves, he wasn't sure that it was the best idea for him to be going off alone again. He wondered if he was in the right mind for all these solo activities that Leah always thought were too dangerous.

Another part of him was thrilled by the danger of it, by the lack of expectations he had.

Already, his adventure had spawned more spontaneity than he had ever found himself prone to before. Even his relationship with Leah had been carefully planned out and assessed from afar. Chris always followed a set path, a track that guided him towards the life he always wanted.

Now that the illusion of a perfect life had been shattered, Chris focused inwardly, scrambling for a different way to guide his decisions.

He followed his gut in this moment, seeking reprieve from his loneliness, yet somehow enjoying it at the same time.

Despite his growing and evolving independence, he still found himself wanting to tell Leah of his personal discoveries, to share with her his adventures in the single life. He could imagine the look of horror on her face as he recounted his time in the sea caves to her, or the fact that he'd now ridden on an elephant.

There was still the physical loneliness that he felt, and he knew that the cure for that was not so simple. He missed the touch of his fiancé, not even the sexual nature of their relationship, but the fact that he could hold her at night as he was falling asleep. He had not held a woman other than Leah before, and he could not imagine doing so.

Serena most certainly did not count, since by any account, she was not real. If he chose to indulge in his *ownership* of her, surely, Leah could take no issue with that. Maybe one day, she would see the truth and realize that Bradley didn't compare to him. Chris would have been the best husband to her, and maybe, he still could be one day.

But for now, all he had was the heart stone in his pocket. He pulled it out as the elephant slowly walked through a patch of shrubbery. He twiddled it in his hands, rubbing the pad of his thumb over the smoothed surface.

He knew it was silly, but he brought it up to his mouth and planted a kiss in the center of it.

For a brief moment, nothing happened, just as he had expected. But soon, that familiar, blinding light began outshining the sun, bursting through the air in radiant, crystalline beams. Chris winced, his chest tightening. He blinked, and when he opened his eyes again, Serena was sitting beside him on the wide saddle.

"Chris," she said in greeting, her voice warm and soft. She gazed at him with tender, affectionate eyes, the same look Leah had given him when he first brought up the idea of marriage to her.

The sight made a lump form in his throat. He still believed her to be nothing more than an apparition, but he enjoyed delighting himself in her beautiful face and angelic voice.

"We're on an elephant," she said observantly.

Chris grinned at her. "We are."

"Did you know that elephants are my favorite animal?" she asked.

It was in that moment that Chris officially decided that she was a figment of his imagination, a sick replication in his mind of the perfect woman he had lost. She was the embodiment of Leah, a more ethereal version of her.

"I did know that," he lied. "That's why I brought us here."

"I've never ridden on an elephant before," she replied. "Aren't they dangerous?"

Chris reached for her hand and clasped her fingers around his. He was almost surprised to find that her body was, in fact, corporeal, a tangible, touchable entity. Her skin was warm and soft. He felt the pressure of her fingers against his as she returned the grasp.

"Don't worry," he told her. "You are perfectly safe here."

She gave him a knowing look, a demure glance

beneath her lashes. "You kissed my heart stone," she said accusingly. "You must have missed me."

Chris felt heat come to his cheeks.

"I did miss you," he said. "Though I'm still not sure exactly what you are."

"*Who*," she corrected. "I am a person."

Chris quirked a brow at her. "Are you?" he demanded. "I don't know any people who live inside tiny stones. It really seems like you may be a product of my own imagination. How else could you materialize beside me like this?"

Serena shook her head ruefully at him, gripping his hand a little tighter.

"You don't understand the heart stone," she argued. "If I am not a person, then why did it feel like I was trapped in there?"

Chris didn't know what to say. It was a step of empathy he had not taken yet, to see her as a person with feelings rather than a ghost haunting his mind.

"I like it here, outside the stone," she continued. "I can feel the sun on my face and your hand around mine. It's nice. The heart stone was nothing like this."

"What *was* the heart stone like?" he pressed.

"Bleak," she replied. "It was a void, but a bright one. Like I was inside a machine."

Chris swallowed the lump in his throat, thumbing

the heart stone in his hands, which apparently was this poor woman's home.

"A machine?" he asked. "What do you mean?"

She looked away from him, a tinge of pink cropping up over the bridge of her nose.

"It's like being plugged into a machine, docked in a state of stasis," she explained. "Like I am dormant and being recharged."

Chris gaped at her, unsure of what to think. When she explained things that way, it put her striking resemblance to Leah in an entirely different light. Who exactly was Serena? If she was not a figment of his imagination, then she must have been something else.

"You're a computer," he said accusingly. "An AI."

Serena nodded, dropping her gaze to her lap. "Can an AI also be a person?" she asked him, keeping her eyes hidden. "I feel like a person. At least, out here I do."

"If you feel like a person, then you are a person," Chris explained. There was not much more to being human than feeling emotion.

"People don't spend an eternity trapped inside a void," she ventured. "I didn't even realize how cold and dark it was in there until you brought me into the sea caves. And now here."

The steps of the elephant rocked and swayed the saddle. As she walked over a particularly uneven part of the ground, Chris clung to his seat for balance. Serena did not seem to mind, and only bounced slightly in her seat.

"That sounds awful," he said, his brows knit together in concern. "How long were you in the stone before I found you?"

She gave a noncommittal shrug. "There was no concept of time in there. I can't say."

"Well, you don't *have* to go back inside," Chris said, confused as to why she never considered this before.

She peered at him with scrutiny, her brown eyes roving and unsure. "You won't make me?" she asked.

Chris gave her a look of bewilderment and shook his head.

"Of course not," he replied. "Who would do something so cruel? Do you think you need to do as I say?"

She gave another shrug, but her gaze was steadier on him now. She flicked it less often to her feet and allowed it to linger more freely on his face.

"You are my owner now."

Chris laughed at her, driving her gaze away from him again. He was amused by the hot red blush on her cheeks, endeared by her sudden shyness.

"Serena, people can't be owned," he explained. "Maybe you *weren't* a person, but you are now. I don't know how you came to be in the heart stone, but you can't be owned outside of it. You never have to go back in there."

She chanced a look back up to his face, her eyes wide and glimmering, reflecting the cotton candy clouds in the blue sky above.

"You mean that?" she asked. "Never?"

"Never," he assured her.

Chapter Seven

True to his word, Chris did not ask Serena to return to the heart stone, even when the elephant had completed her circuit, and they were ambling back into the animal sanctuary. He had no explanation planned for her mysterious appearance. He hoped to leave quickly after disembarking and get Serena to somewhere a little safer.

Her glow was less apparent in the afternoon sun, but Chris still noticed when he squinted that there was something faintly radiant about her skin.

When they returned the elephant to its coral, the guide had a profound look of confusion on his face. He asked Chris who she was, but he brushed off the question. Flustered, he helped Serena down off the saddle, and she wrapped her arm around his as they made their way back to the entrance. He was just glad to know that others could see Serena too, that he wasn't just imagining her.

They easily slipped into the crowd of people. Serena let out a giggle of delight beside him that sent a skittering pleasure down his spine.

"Where are we going now?" she asked. He loved the sense of wonder he could see on her face, her sheer happiness that was obvious from the eye-crinkling way she smiled.

"Where do you want to go, Serena?" he asked.

She tapped her finger against her mouth, pondering. Chris watched with a smile on his face, captivated by every facet of her beauty, from her glimmering eyes to her pursed, pink lips.

"I think I'm hungry," she finally said.

"You think?"

She nodded.

"Then let's get something to eat."

They headed back to Phuket in a cab, crowded together in the back seat. Serena did not want to take her hands off him, as if he might disappear if she didn't touch him at all times. Her hip was always pressed against his, her arm looped tightly around his elbow. She leaned her head against his shoulder and released a sigh.

Unable to resist, Chris leaned down to sniff her hair. She smelled like fresh cloves of cinnamon and something faintly sweet and unidentifiable.

"Chris?" she asked him, her voice a hushed whisper.

"Yes, darling?" he replied.

"I'm feeling new things," she said. "Things I've never felt before. Can I describe them to you? I want to understand them."

"Yes, please do," he urged her. Her personhood was still somewhat in question, and he would take any chance he could get to understand her more.

She lifted a long, elegant finger and pointed through the window, where they could both see a line of acacia trees whizzing past.

"I feel like the tops of those trees," she said. "The way they sway in the wind, still tethered to the ground. How the sun mutes my skin... it makes me feel small. I felt so big in the heart stone, like *I* was the universe."

Chris rubbed soothingly at her arm.

"You are out here now," he said consolingly. "We're all small out here, compared to the universe. Now, you can know what it feels like to be small and unsteady like the rest of us."

"Will you be by my side while I learn how to feel all these new things?" she asked, tilting her face on his shoulder to look up at him.

"Of course, I will," he said, pressing a chaste kiss to her forehead.

For the rest of his stay in Thailand, Serena was persistently by Chris's side. It reminded him of how clingy Leah had been right after they left high school. He had gone to college, grown into his features, and she grew jealous as she stayed behind to go to culinary school. That distance between them during those years always bothered her, and during that time, she had always been physically affectionate with him in an almost desperate sort of way.

Serena was no less desperate now. Chris could tell that she was quickly absorbing new experiences, letting them shape her new perceptions of the world.

He showed her what Phuket had to offer, taking her to try different kinds of cuisine, watching her graceful attempt at windsurfing. Despite her unwieldy emotional state, she seemed adept with the physical nature of the world: athletic, nimble, and lithe.

There was something inherently romantic about

the whole venture, and Chris was worried that when he returned to America, Serena would disappear. It was almost like a fairy tale, watching Serena discover herself like this at the exotic beaches of Phuket. Would either of them be the same after they return home?

He pondered this when he booked an extra plane ticket for her.

It wasn't just that she'd be too perfect to exist. There were many other logistical questions to reckon with. This woman had no family, no identity beyond the heart stone he kept stored in his pocket at all times. She would need to get an ID, apply for insurance, and build herself a normal life in the human world from scratch.

By the time they finished sitting through the twenty-four-hour flight, Serena seemed very aware of how much of a burden her existence was. The airport was a scary place for her, evidenced by her saucer-round eyes and the clammy fist she kept wrapped tightly around his hand. She was beginning to see the common struggles of the average person, the hustling through busy crowds, waiting in long lines.

She was very flustered by the time they arrived at his house. He took note of her shivering as he urged her through the front door and into the dark living room.

"Are you cold?" he asked, reaching for the throw

blanket Leah had left draped across the back of the couch. He wrapped it around her shoulders when she nodded.

"The air here is different than Thailand's," she said.

Chris smiled at her. "Yeah, it's much colder here. You'll get used to it."

"Will I get used to these other feelings?" she asked. "Sometimes I get this feeling in my stomach, like there are butterflies fluttering around in there. What does it mean?"

Chris canted his head to one side and stared at her curiously.

"Is it a pleasant feeling or an unpleasant one?" he asked.

Serena let out a hum as she thought of how to describe it.

"Both," she finally replied. "Or one or the other, rather. Sometimes it's very unpleasant, like when we were at the airport, and we kept having to rush around to where we were supposed to be. It was like I had a stomach full of bees, just gnawing away at my insides."

Chris let out a chuckle of amusement.

"And other times?" he pressed.

That agreeable flush returned to her cheeks, dusting across the bridge of her nose and even down her neck. He remembered how red Leah had been the first time he kissed her, how the redness had splayed all the way down to her chest.

"Other times, it's an entirely different sensation, yet, it still makes my insides feel like jelly," she explained. "It's like a warm, bubbling, sparkling feeling. It's wonderful, really. I wish I knew how to describe it better."

Chris tucked a single strand of hair away from her face.

"When do you feel like that?" he asked.

She averted her gaze, drawing her lower lip in between her pearly teeth.

"Every time I look at you," she answered.

The sensation she had just described to him suddenly invaded his senses. He could not help but smile at her, relieved to hear that she was developing stronger kinds of feelings. He could already feel himself falling in love with her, and it comforted him to know that she might be able to return the same feeling.

He framed her face with his hands and leaned down to kiss her on the lips. He could feel her pulse beating wildly beneath his palm, and he was sure his own heart was racing just as fast. She tasted sweet, like the lemon candies she had been eating on the plane. Her lips were soft and supple beneath his, and he felt a heated pleasure coiling in his gut.

"Chris," she said, breaking away from him by

pushing lightly at his chest. "Are you sure I'm not too much of a burden on you? To open your home to me like this... I don't want to inconvenience you. I belong in the heart stone, you know."

A noise of disgust escaped from the back of his throat.

"You are *not* going back in the heart stone," he insisted. "I want you here with me. You aren't a burden at all. It would be my pleasure if you let me take care of you."

Serena grinned at him and threw her arms around his neck.

"Thank you, Chris," she murmured in his ear. "I feel like I'm becoming a real person because of you. I'm glad the heart stone found its way to you."

"Me too, Serena," he replied and leaned down for another kiss.

Chapter Eight

Serena adapted easily to the world around her. Life as Chris knew it before the breakup returned relatively quickly. With Serena at his side, he felt lighter than air. Though he had been unaware of Leah's unhappiness with the relationship, there was no mistaking Serena's. She was truly delighted to be with him and fell easily into the role of his girlfriend.

It became entirely irrelevant to Chris that she was an AI. As she learned to develop her emotions and feelings, she became more and more like a person. Her flaws began to crop up, not marring her perfection but improving it. He liked her better with the stain of humanity on her, the ability to get frustrated and make mistakes. It humbled him...in a way.

Desperate to earn her keep in his home, Serena cooked and cleaned for him while he was away at work. His shirts were always neatly pressed, and though her cooking wasn't quite as delicious as Leah's was, it's always made with his tastes and preferences in mind.

He wondered sometimes if she still believed that he was her owner. The thought unsettled him, knowing what a responsibility he had to make sure not to abuse her fragile state. Her personhood always seemed up for debate, at least in her mind. She was constantly fretting over whether she was "human" enough.

Chris saw the humanity in her every day. She had an extraordinary empathy, that at first only seemed to extend to him. She was never unkind to anyone, but sometimes, it seemed like the Earth orbited around Chris, that she could think of nothing but him.

Yet, as he shared more of his life and the world with her, she began to notice the people around her more. She asked questions to the waiters at restaurants or the cashier at the grocery store. Chris could tell that her eagerness was off-putting to some people who found her questions personal and invasive. She never seemed to want to ask about the weather, but always about the last time a person had cried or if they have ever lost a loved one.

Eventually, the newness of life wore off for her, and neither of them had any doubts that she was a person. She could connect so easily to anybody she met now, like she had not just discovered all the different human conditions that could exist but absorbed them into herself. When others were happy, so was Serena.

It was the quality that Chris loved the most about her. He had loved that same quality in Leah, though not to this almost debilitating degree. He had to be careful with his emotions, especially those like anger or fear or sadness. She reflected them back as if they were her own, and in order to keep her happy, Chris learned to control his emotions better.

After a few months of living together in a perfect, warm, domestic bliss, Chris decided to propose to Serena. She was perfect in a way that even Leah was not, someone made to fit beside him and love him. He had no idea what luck would come to him on that flippant trip to Thailand, but he knew now that he did not want to live without her.

He was nervous the day he came home from work with an engagement ring in his pocket. The one that Leah had given back to him had been returned, and he used that money to buy another one, a simpler pearl engagement ring that he thought suited Serena well. Leah would never have been satisfied with anything other than a diamond, but Chris knew that Serena would be delighted with the pearl, that it would complement her elegance and grace more beautifully than a diamond ever could.

She was setting the table for dinner when he walked through the kitchen door. The smell of roasted chicken wafted through the air, and Serena had poured them each a glass of white wine. She beamed at him as he greeted her with a kiss on the cheek and sat down at the table.

"How was work today?" she asked him as she pulled the steaming pan of fish out of the oven. She set it down on top of the stove and fanned at it with her oven mitt.

Chris stared at her, enchanted by her graceful movements even when doing mundane things. He imagined her with his ring around her finger, swollen with his child in her belly. He could not wait to start a life with her, to make her his wife.

He had wanted to wait until after dinner so he could set the mood with candles and soft music while she went to freshen up, but he was too eager. He knew there were grander ways to propose to a woman, but there was something about the simplicity of this that spoke to him. To Chris, Serena *was* home, and to propose to her here symbolized how much he felt like she belonged here.

"Serena," he said, clearing his throat. She turned to face him as he wiped his clammy hands on his pants leg and reached into his pocket for the ring box.

She saw it immediately, her eyes locked onto where he held it in his trembling fingers. Her hands flew to cover her mouth, her eyes wide with shock. Nervously, Chris approached her and stooped down onto one knee.

"Serena, my love," he said, his voice quaking with emotion. "You mean the absolute world to me. The best day of my life was the day you rescued me from those caves. I have never been this happy with anyone before, and I didn't think that was possible. I can't live without you, Serena. I want you to be my wife. I want to spend the rest of my life with you."

A loud, rattling peal of thunder suddenly shook the windows. Chris and Serena both flicked their gazes to the splatter of rain against the glass. Their gazes drifted back to each other, both of them wearing sheepish smiles.

"I would love to be your wife, Chris," she said,

pulling him back up to his feet so she could wrap her arms around him in an affectionate embrace.

He lifted her off her feet and kissed her, his chest swelling with a warm bubble of happiness. He was eager to begin the next chapter of his life with her, to put everything else behind him.

She pulled away from him to press feverish kisses all over his face, beaming from ear to ear whenever her lips were not pressed to his. Finally, he removed the ring from its velvet enclosure and placed it on her manicured finger. Serena held her pale, beautiful hand up to the light and wiggled her fingers, admiring the precious stone.

"A pearl," she cooed. "It's lovely, Chris."

She pulled him into another kiss, threading her fingers into the curls at the nape of his neck. Chris held her against him, his hands sliding to her waist. He felt the first stirrings of desire for her and deepened their kiss.

As his hands began to wander further, Serena latched her fingers around his wrists and gently pushed him away with a laugh.

"After dinner," she assured him with a final, chaste peck on the lips. "I worked hard on this halibut. Let's not let it get cold."

Chris gave a sheepish laugh of agreement and

resumed his place at the kitchen table. His cheeks ached with the strain of the permanent smile adhered to his face. Serena bustled around the kitchen, fetching silverware and removing simmering vegetables from the stove. Chris watched her, his eyes drawn toward the ring on her finger and the sweet sway of her narrow hips.

They enjoyed her roasted halibut and drank wine, sharing in their happiness with one another. Chris didn't have a care in the world when he was with Serena. Laughter flowed through him in her presence, an eruption of the magnanimous joy he felt at every moment by her side.

Later that night, as they were slipping into bed, Chris removed the heart stone that had been burning a hole in his pocket all day. It seemed like a strange relic to keep sometimes, like a totem he hung onto with little reason. The longer Serena was out of it, the less it felt like the magical artifact that it was. He wondered what would happen to Serena if she separated from it permanently. He never really understood what she meant when she said she felt like she was docked to a machine inside the stone. *Did* it recharge her? Was the computer side of her fading as her human side took over?

The reality was that the heart stone was merely a piece of glass, at least, now it was. He set it down on the dresser and turned to look at Serena, who had already slipped beneath the covers of the bed.

"Do you think I should do something with the heart stone?" he asked her. It was the place of *her* origination, after all, so the choice should be hers.

"Like what?" she asked, flipping onto her side to face him as he slid into the spot beside her. She sank against his side, falling into his gravity, the dip he created in the mattress.

He let out a puff of air as he thought about his response.

"We should get rid of it, don't you think?" he asked. "I don't want you to accidentally touch it and get sucked back inside."

Serena shook her head, throwing one arm over his chest. She splayed her hand over his heart as if claiming it, the pearl on her finger glinting in the low lamplight.

"I couldn't bear to get rid of it," she said. "I feel like it's a part of me."

"You're right," Chris murmured in agreement. "Perhaps we should put it in a shadowbox and hang it over the mantle."

Serena was more approving of that idea.

"Perhaps," she said. "As long as no one else touches it. I'm afraid of what might happen if it were to fall into another person's hands. You've been kind enough to give me freedom, but others might abuse the power of the heart stone. I wouldn't want anything to come between us like that."

Chris hadn't considered that about the heart stone. The ownership aspect of things had always confused him. If another person kissed the stone while Serena was out of it, would she be forced to leave Chris? Or did she have to be inside the stone for the kiss to work? Perhaps it *would* be best to keep the stone in a safe place. If he was being honest with himself, he still wanted to keep it in his pocket.

"No, I wouldn't want that either," he said, dropping a kiss on top of her head.

Chapter Nine

A few weeks passed since Chris had proposed, and he was eager to set a date for the wedding. After his experience with Leah, he was uninterested in a long engagement. Unlike many of his peers from college who were already married, Chris wanted to be an avid participant in the wedding planning.

This worked out well in Serena's favor, who had never planned a social event in her life. She didn't even have family to invite, though over her short life with Chris in America so far, she had made many friends with her effervescent personality.

One night, after they had spent most of the evening choosing fabrics for the tables at the wedding, Chris took Serena downtown for a celebratory date. They took the cobblestone path from the house and cruised down the bustling streets.

Serena was childlike as they ambled down the path, pointing at flowers and weeds growing from the cracks between the cobblestone, and swaying her hips to music when they passed a loud bar. They arrived at the main square, and Serena pointed across the street.

"Look at that couple," she said with a sigh. "Don't they look sweet?"

"Not as sweet as us," he said teasingly as he glanced across the street at them.

His blood ran icy cold through his veins when he saw Leah's restaurant across the street. She was standing outside the entrance, her arms wrapped around the neck of the man Chris knew to be Bradley. He watched him kiss her on the lips and felt the first pang of jealousy that he'd felt in a while.

He'd mentioned Leah only in passing to Serena. She couldn't possibly understand how hard it was for him to see Leah like this, and he didn't want her to know.

Still, it was impossible for him to hide the look of agitation on his face, so when he felt Serena's hand land on his arm in concern, he dragged his gaze to her face and swallowed the lump in his throat.

"What's wrong?" she asked, peering up at him with her round, concerned eyes. "Are you alright? You look like you just saw a ghost."

Chris shook his head and placed his hand on the small of her back to resume leading her down the street.

"I'm okay," he insisted. "Just thinking of a memory."

"A bad one?" she pressed.

Chris nodded. "Kind of," he said. "Remembering it makes me sad."

Serena fell silent for a moment, lost in her thoughts. Chris glanced back over his shoulder to see that Leah and Bradley were gone.

"What did it feel like to be sad?" she asked.

Chris grimaced. It was one thing to help her understand the lovelier emotions a person could feel. To explain sadness and anger and fear was much harder. He wished she would never even think of those things and just be content to be happy all the time.

But he'd gotten to know her well over the last few

months, and Chris knew how insatiably curious Serena could be.

"It's the opposite of happiness," he explained. "Sorrow. Dread. Like pain in your heart, but not your real heart. Like your soul."

"My soul?"

He nodded again. "It's a terrible feeling, Serena," he explained. "I hope you never have to experience anything like it."

Serena's footsteps faltered. She cocked her head to the side and looked at him with a furrowed brow, her lips pursed together.

"I think I *have* felt what it's like to be sad," she confessed, twisting her fingers together nervously. "Is that what it means to be human? To have a soul? Oh, Chris, do you think I have a soul?"

Chris frowned at her. "When were you sad?" he demanded, though not harshly.

"I felt it for the first time when I saw a squirrel get run over by a car last week," she told him, "and again when I went to make you your favorite dinner, but we were out of milk for the gravy."

Chris gave her a perplexed look and hoped that was the extent of any sadness she ever felt. He couldn't know what it was like for emotions to be so new, and he wanted to laugh at her, but he knew it would provoke more questions.

"Come on, darling," he said, pulling her into a strong hug and kissing the top of her head. "Let's forget about being sad for now."

Over the next few days, Serena seemed to lose the cheerful smile she always wore. There was something behind her eyes that was undeniably human, a look Chris couldn't remember seeing there ever before.

He knew exactly what it was. Sadness. The real

kind. Serena was not as good at hiding it as most people were. He was dying to know *why* she had developed this new emotion, and what had brought it about. Yet, he couldn't bring himself to ask her. There was something traumatic about seeing that expression on her face, the very same one Leah had worn when she gave him the ring back.

So, Chris did the logical thing and ignored it. Instead of addressing it directly, he bought her flowers on the way home from work and massaged her feet at night before they fell asleep. He was quick to assure her that he loved her, to shower her with praise and affection, trying to bring those happy feelings bubbling back up to the surface.

Sometimes it seemed to be working, but Chris still felt something gnawing away at the bond he had forged between them. He had an overwhelming desire to shield her from everything in the world but him, anything that would program her against him. With nauseating shame, he briefly contemplated putting her back into the heart stone and letting her "recharge," as she had put it.

He didn't want Serena to slip away the same way Leah had.

One day, Chris came home from work to find Serena crying. He had never seen her cry before, and the sight of her with glassy eyes and a heaving chest hit him like a bolt of lightning.

"Serena, darling, what's the matter?" he asked, rushing to her side.

She shrugged away from his touch, much to his dismay. She wrapped her arms around herself, folding herself as small as she could make herself be.

"I'm sad, Chris," she said through her thick tears. "It made my eyes wet and my soul hurt. My soul *really* hurts."

"What happened?" he breathed, not sure that he wanted to know the answer.

"I've been out of the heart stone for a long time now," she said. "It used to stop me from feeling all these things. Sometimes I would get an inkling of a feeling, but when I went back into the stone, it was erased like it never happened."

Chris took a shaky breath and pulled her over to the sofa. With tender hands, he sat her down, rubbing the tears on her cheeks away with his thumb.

"It's overwhelming, I'm sure," he said patiently. "You'll get used to these feelings, love. No one said it was easy to be human."

She let out a watery laugh. "Did you know that there's a man at the grocery store with one arm?" she asked. "He told me he lost it in Iraq. And there's a woman I met at the library who is in love with *two* men. She's pregnant and doesn't know which one is the father."

Chris knit his brows together, unsure of what to say.

"On Wednesdays, at the farmers market, a group of actors get together to perform Shakespeare's plays," she continued. "The emotions I see on their faces are so real. It's hard to imagine that they are faking them. I don't think I can do that. How can I pretend to feel a way I've never felt before?"

The blood in Chris's veins grew ice cold as her words began to swim in his head. He couldn't really understand her point. He only knew that her raw tears were brewing up a sense of dread in his stomach.

"You make me happy, Chris, but there are so many other things I want to feel."

Chris instinctively shook his head. He licked his dry lips and sucked in a deep breath for patience.

"You'll feel it all in time, Serena," he said. "You can't rush the human experience."

"Part of the human experience is being able to make my own choices," she argued. "I love you, Chris, but you are still the owner of the heart stone. I can't truly be free when I am with you."

Chris glared at her, appalled that she would even think such a thing.

"You *are* free," he insisted. "I would *never* make you go back in there. You know that."

"I know," she agreed. "That's why I know you'll let me go back to Thailand. Alone."

Chris blinked at her, too afraid his tongue wouldn't work if he tried to speak.

"You gave me my personhood, Chris," she continued, wiping at her tears with the back of her hand. "I'll always be grateful for that. But I'll always wonder if you're still my owner, if what I feel is actually *real*. I want to know for sure. I want to feel things with other people and explore the world. I don't think I'm ready to settle down with you. There's still so much I have left to experience."

Chris's chest felt so tight he thought he might have stopped breathing. His blood was roaring in his ears, his fingers quaking at his side. He yearned to reach out and touch her cheek, to pull her against him and pretend she'd said nothing at all.

But the tears on her face were unmistakable, and her pain was obvious. It made him sick to see it, and even sicker to know that he had been the one holding her back.

"I'll take you to Thailand," he finally replied. "You don't have to go alone. We can explore together, just you and me."

Serena shook her head.

"You should have kept me in the heart stone, Chris," she said with regret. "This would have never happened."

Now, it was Chris's turn to shake his head.

"No, Serena," he said sincerely. "I'm glad I've kept you out of the heart stone. You *are* a real person, and nothing can change that now."

She blinked up at him, tears still clinging to her lashes.

"So, does that mean I'm really free?" she asked.

Chris stood frozen, his mouth suddenly very dry. Serena was waiting for his reply with wavering eyes, the engagement ring still tucked in her clenched fist. He did not want to let her go, and yet, he knew he could not force her to stay.

"You were never my prisoner, Serena."

She nodded solemnly and sniffled. Her hand came up to his, and he felt her press the ring into his palm.

"Thank you," she said earnestly. "I see that this hurts you, and that makes me so much sadder. But beneath that, I'm really happy that I met you and got to know you. You've done more for me than you could possibly imagine."

"I wish I did enough to make you stay," he murmured.

A quiet sob escaped her. Chris knew her emotions were still raw and overwhelming, so he wrapped her in his arms and held her tightly against him, probably for the very last time. He was sure she could hear his heart pounding in his chest.

"You should take the heart stone with you," he murmured as she sobbed into his chest. "I'll wrap it up well for you so you don't accidentally touch it."

"No," she said sharply, even through her tears. She pulled back just far enough to look at him, gripping his arms with trembling fingers. "I want you to keep it. You're the only person I trust to have it."

Chris's heart twisted in his chest. If she trusted him so much, then why was that not enough? He was not enough for Leah, and as it turned out, not enough for Serena either. He could not figure out what he was doing wrong, and he felt the pain of his failure.

"Keep it, and remember me," she insisted.

Chris wasn't sure he wanted to remember her after this.

"I'll never forget you, Chris," she told him, and she leaned up to give him one last goodbye kiss.

That night, after Serena had packed up what few belongings she had and fled out into the world, Chris sat alone in his bedroom. The room was dark, the blinds drawn. The ceiling fan overhead whirred rhythmically in the darkness, a thrumming, persistent reminder of his loneliness.

The heart stone was clutched in his fist, weighing

heavily against his chest where he held it. He had thought about walking down to the river and tossing the stone into the water, but right now, he couldn't let go of it.

By giving Serena her humanity, he had also given her the ability to break his heart. He couldn't be mad at her for choosing to exercise the freedom he had given her. It was his foolish mistake for falling in love with an AI, for making the same mistakes with her as he had with Leah.

As he reflected back on his time with both of them, he couldn't help but feel like his only real mistake had been being blind to their unhappiness. He found it hard to recognize his own sometimes, choosing to ignore it rather than addressing it. Perhaps, that was where it had all gone so wrong. He saw what *he* wanted to see.

Regardless of how they had broken his heart, Chris wished nothing but the best for both Leah and Serena. He wanted them to find fulfillment in life, to achieve everything they ever wanted.

None of that quelled the pain in his own heart though. He closed his eyes and slowly brought the heart stone up to his lips. The stone was smooth and warm where he kissed it, and he thought he felt a bright light swelling in the room.

But when he opened his eyes again, it was still dark, and he was still alone.

The End

About the Author

Viola Tempest is a dystopian fantasy and paranormal romance author who yearns to expose the truth of those in the modern world: the good, the bad, and the ugly. Her inspiration primarily stems from life experiences, those who annoy her, ex-boyfriends, and the crazy dreams that pop into her head every once in a while.

Stalk her below!

* * *

Website:
https://www.violatempest.com/

Facebook Page:
https://www.facebook.com/authorviolatempest

Instagram:
https://www.instagram.com/author_violatempest/

Goodreads:
https://www.goodreads.com/author/show/21693342.
Viola_Tempest

Bookbub:
https://www.bookbub.com/authors/viola-tempest

Shattered Heart

ENCHANTED WISHES COLLECTION

VIOLA TEMPEST